FOREWORD

In January 2015, I was four years out of college. I worked three day jobs and a writing gig that ate up my nights. I lived with my family and desperately struggled to pull together a comics portfolio. At twenty-five years old, I was nowhere nearer my dream of publication than I was at eight years old when I decided to head down this path. When Nechama Frier dropped into my house and asked if I was interested in creating an anthology with her, it felt like the sun rising. When we settled on a theme—an anthology of fiends!—I felt like the way forward was completely clear.

We've been blessed at every turn with abundance: nearly 150 submissions to our call for entries, 22 incredible creators at the final draw, a spectacular last-minute push to get the book funded—even the simple benefit of having two editors to share the load threw light on every step of the journey.

From the start, we had the help of friends: Kath Hsi saved us from ourselves with her elegant, nuanced design from day one; Luke Blackwood committed hours and hours of his expertise to creating and cutting the Kickstarter video; and Jeff Moore's role as the coolest chauffeur on the East Coast helped bridge the Baltimore to Ithaca distance in an invaluable way. Without these people, this project would have been poorer and (let's face it) probably a lot less attractive.

And of course, we can't offer enough thanks to all of our Kickstarter backers, dedicated, passionate readers and creators yourselves. We were completely blown away by not only the eleventh hour rush to the finish line, but also the zeal with which you all shared this project with your friends. Special thanks to Michelle Czajkowski, Mary Nann, Marci Cancio-Bello, J. Cope, Sam Kennedy, David Gallaher, and Trystan Vel for their enthusiastic support!

In January 2016, I've made a few changes in my life, the most significant of which being the book you're reading now: my first printed book. With so little to show for my ambitions at the start of this endeavor, I feel doubly proud to have collected these incredibly creators and to present my work alongside them. We've all gotten dirty to find these diamonds, but the stories in this collection are beautiful, sharp, and strong as any gem. Being part of this brilliant cluster has strengthened and sharpened my life, too. As this book goes out into the world, I get to go out with it, richer in work and experience for having made the thing, richer in spirit for having made it with Nechama and this dazzling array of creators.

All the time, all the energy, all the money comes to a head here. We are so grateful for all your help, and we hope that this collection brings you what it's brought to us: joy, inspiration, and a little bit of the spooks!

YOURS,
TEN VAN WINKLE

Published by Nechama Frier and Ten Van Winkle
Printed in Canada by WEBCOM Inc.

Cover illustration by Lynn Nguyen
Design by Kath Hsi

FIRST EDITION February 2016
ISBN 978-0-692-62421-0

VERTO

SCOPE

TABLE OF CONTENTS

THE DEVIL'S DENTIST
悪魔の歯医者

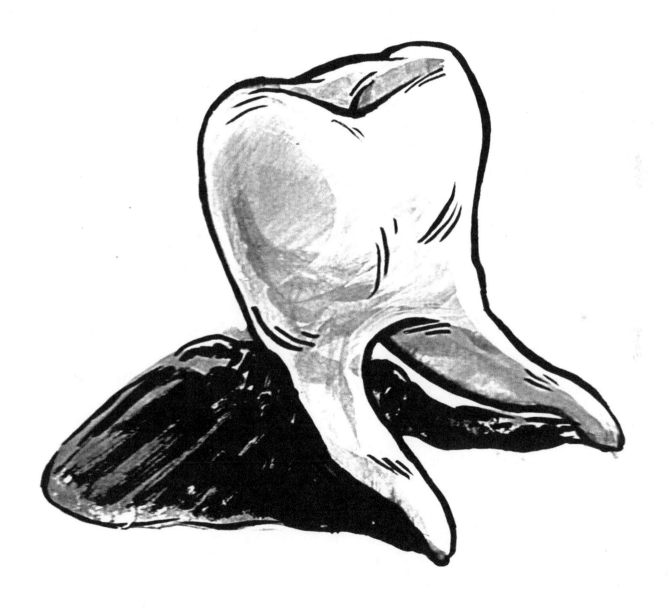

BY MADY G.
www.madyg.com

INSPIRED BY THE WORK OF JUNJI ITO.

TEETH LAY SCATTERED AT THE EDGE OF THE WOOD.

SMALL AND AND BRIGHT LIKE PEBBLES

SOME OF MY CLASSMATES SAY A DEVILISH WOLF LIVES THERE. . .

SOME SAY IT'S A MEETING SPOT FOR SOME SORT OF SATANIC CULT . . .

EITHER WAY . . .

TOWNSPEOPLE HAVE BEEN DISAPPEARING INTO THAT WOOD FOR ABOUT THREE MONTHS NOW.

YUKO, ALWAYS THE IM-
PULSIVE ONE, WANTED
TO SEE WHAT THE FUSS
WAS ABOUT.

HARU WENT ALONG TOO
BECAUSE SHE ALWAYS
LISTENED TO YUKO.

CHIBA ALSO TAGGED
BEHIND BECAUSE SHE
HAD NOWHERE ELSE
TO GO.

I KNEW
IT WAS A BAD IDEA
SO I FOLLOWED TOO.

TEETH DOTTED THE GRASS AND BRUSH LIKE FIREFLIES.

THREE OF US HUGGED THE WOOD'S EDGE WITH OUR TOES.

YUKO HUNG FROM THE BRANCHES AND SHOUTED,

あはははは〜はは〜

CHICKEN! YOU GUYS ARE SO CHICKEN!

あはははははは〜

TYPICAL YUKO...

THE SKY WAS A SMALL RIP BETWEEN
THE CRAGGY TREETOPS.
THE FOREST FLOOR WAS DAMP AND SMELLED OF SMOKE AND
PETRICHOR.
NO BIRDS SANG AND EVEN THE DEER WOULDN'T PASS THE
OUTSKIRTS.

WE WERE ALONE AND THIS WOULD BE OUR PLAYGROUND.

YUKO, OF COURSE, WAS THE LEADER OF THE GAME.

WE WOULD ALL HIDE AND WAIT FOR HARU TO FIND US.

HARU AGREED BECAUSE SHE ALWAYS LISTENED TO YUKO.

SHE COUNTED TO 60 AND WE VANISHED ONE BY ONE BETWEEN THE TRUNKS.

AT LEAST 20 MINUTES PASSED, MAYBE MORE AS I WAITED, CONCEALED BY THE BUSHES...

...BEFORE A SUDDEN SCREAM SPLIT THE SILENCE LIKE A KNIFE.

I HURRIEDLY RETURNED TO THE BIG TREE WHERE I SAW YUKO AND CHIBA GATHERED.

HARU'S BODY LAY, TOOTHLESS MAW RIPPED ASUNDER BY NAMELESS CLAWS.

CHIBA WAS SICK

YUKO ARMED HERSELF

AND I BOLTED.

THE MORE I RAN, THE DEEPER I FOUND MYSELF IN A MAZE OF TREES.

ANOTHER SCREAM TORE THROUGH THE UNDERBRUSH AND I KNEW THAT CHIBA HAD BEEN TAKEN.

I IMAGINED THE DEVIL WOLF RIPPING HER YOUNG BODY TO SHREDS...

I PRESSED ON IN A PANIC.

9

I SAW A LIGHT UP AHEAD AND A WAVE OF RELIEF RUSHED OVER ME...

COULD IT BE?

THE EDGE OF THIS HELL?

FREEDOM?

I BURST FORTH FROM THE WILD BUSHES.

WHAT I SAW THEN... I CAN'T DESCRIBE—

おわり。 12

Once, in a land of forgotten stories, there was a living puppet weary of playing the fool...

...and an honest man who could never reap what he'd sown.

When they realized Fate did not favour them, they escaped the relentless cycles of their Stories to strike out better fortunes.

Together, they became renegade treasure hunters, so they may possess what their Stories denied them.

One day, they reached the town of the Clever Tailor.

A bear with a lethal gaze stalked the tailor's poor townsfolk. But, armed with a needle that can stitch anything, the Clever Tailor sewed up the bear's eyes while she was asleep.

The townsfolk honored the Tailor as their hero, and he retired his business to become their vigilant watchman.

He knew better than to engage her in combat, and so led her to an old shed and set it aflame.

But a magic needle always draws attention, particularly the sights of a certain pair of treasure hunters...

16

17

YOU TWO!

WHAT ARE YOU DOING IN THESE WOODS?

ANOTHER TAILOR? YOU SHOULD BE IN TOWN WITH THE OTHER TOWNSFOLK.

IT'S NOT SAFE OUT HERE.

...

OH! DO I HAVE THE GOOD FORTUNE OF ADDRESSING THE CLEVER TAILOR?

YES...

I'VE HEARD OF YOUR SKILLS AND SOUGHT YOU OUT, LOOKING FOR WORK. I WOULD BE HONOURED IF YOU'D HELP ME BETTER MY CRAFT!

OF COURSE I CAN HELP YOU...

BUT WHO'S HE? A TRAVELLING ACTOR?

...

I HAVEN'T THE FAINTEST IDEA. I JUST FOUND HIM LIKE THIS.

!!!

18

WHY, YOU SWINE! YOU BLOODY TRAITOR!

I WANT TO HELP HIM, BUT I'M AFRAID HE'LL ASK FOR MONEY ONCE I DO.

I WON'T TOLERATE WANDERING BEGGARS.

MARTE! HANNES! ARREST HIM!

AND DRAG HIM BACK TO TOWN? THE BEAR MAY ESCAPE IF WE DON'T RETURN QUICKLY WITH THE KINDLING.

LOCK HIM IN WITH THE BEAR, THEN.

OOH, HOW EXCITING!

HEY! NO, WAIT! HANDS OFF, YOU THUGS!

YOU'LL PAY FOR THIS ONE, SHEARS!

YOU'LL HAVE UNTIL SUNSET, WHEN THE SHED BURNS. MAKE PEACE WITH YOURSELF BY THEN.

TCH...

WHO'S THERE? HAS SOMEONE COME TO FEED ME?

OH...NO! YOU COULDN'T POSSIBLY EAT ME. I'M MADE OF WOOD. I'M NOT A LIVING CREATURE AT ALL!

YOU'RE LYING. I CAN SMELL YOU. YOU MUST BE MY LAST MEAL, THEN.

...AH.

MAYBE I SHOULD TURN TO WOOD LIKE OL' SHEARS SAYS.

THE BEAR WOULDN'T EAT ME, AND I COULD TAKE MY LEG APART AND GET OUT OF THESE CHAINS TOO...

...

OH, WELL.

I SUPPOSE I HAD AS GOOD OF A LIFE AS ANY, GIVEN MY UNFORTUNATE POSITION. NO ONE MOURNS THE FOOL, SO I'LL HAVE TO PLAY MY OWN FUNERAL DIRGE.

THAT'S A PRETTY SOUND.

HEH. I'M A TRIFLER AT IT, REALLY.

YOU'RE THE DEADLY BEAR, I TAKE IT? THE PINNACLE OF THE TAILOR'S CAREER...

I WAS A LOT LIKE YOU, YOU KNOW.

HOW? WERE YOU TREATED LIKE AN ANIMAL?

NOT QUITE. BUT IN MY STORY, I HAD TO PLAY THE FOOL SO A KNIGHT COULD BE THE SHINING HERO. IT'S THE SAME HERE TOO. WITHOUT YOU, THAT TAILOR WOULD STILL BE A POOR MAN, RESPECTED BY NOBODY.

ISN'T IT FUNNY?

THE GOOD ONES CAN'T BE HEROIC ON THEIR OWN. THEY NEED SOMEONE ELSE TO MISBEHAVE FIRST. AND YET THEY STILL DAMN US FOR WHAT WE DO.

21

THAT'S WHY I ESCAPED MY STORY. AT LEAST YOU'RE NOT DAMNED TO BE A HYPOCRITE WHEN YOU'RE THE VILLAIN.

BUT YOU WERE STILL SAD TO LEAVE.

WHAT?! OF COURSE NOT! IT WAS GOOD RIDDANCE FOR ALL PARTIES INVOLVED.

YOU HUMANS LIE WITH YOUR WORDS ALL OF THE TIME, BUT YOUR MUSIC HIDES NOTHING.

...

WOULD YOU LIKE A TRY? I'M SURE YOU CAN PLAY JUST AS WELL AS I CAN.

I CAN'T. I'LL BREAK YOUR LUTE WITH MY CLAWS. THEY BREAK ALMOST EVERYTHING.

AH, HA! LUCKY FOR YOU, I HAVE A RATHER LARGE PAIR OF SCISSORS WITH ME. I'LL TRIM YOUR NAILS FOR YOU, FREE OF CHARGE, AS A FAVOUR.

THINK OF IT AS A GIFT FROM ONE DOWNTRODDEN CREATURE TO ANOTHER.

WHAT'S THAT SOUND?

ARE YOU TAKING OUT THE SCISSORS NOW?

22

GRRRRAAAAHHH!!!

DEARY ME! WAS THAT THE BEAR?

OH, NO! THERE'S NO TIME TO COLLECT KINDLING NOW! IF WE DON'T HURRY, SHE'LL ESCAPE!

AH... BEFORE YOU BURN THAT SHED UP...

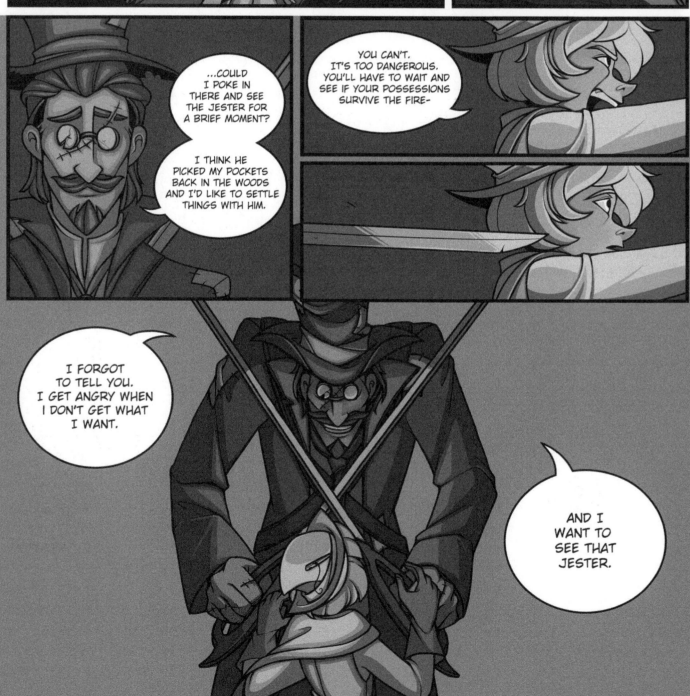

...COULD I POKE IN THERE AND SEE THE JESTER FOR A BRIEF MOMENT?

I THINK HE PICKED MY POCKETS BACK IN THE WOODS AND I'D LIKE TO SETTLE THINGS WITH HIM.

YOU CAN'T. IT'S TOO DANGEROUS. YOU'LL HAVE TO WAIT AND SEE IF YOUR POSSESSIONS SURVIVE THE FIRE—

I FORGOT TO TELL YOU. I GET ANGRY WHEN I DON'T GET WHAT I WANT.

AND I WANT TO SEE THAT JESTER.

24

AAARRRGGHH!!!

PHEW! SHE CAN'T EAT ME NOW.

YOU HUMANS ARE ALL THE SAME!

SHE REALLY DOESN'T KNOW WHERE I AM. WHY CAN'T SHE SMELL ME?

WAIT. I SMELL THAT TOO. IT'S SMOKE.

DAMN! THE SHED'S ON FIRE ALREADY?

IF I TURN INTO WOOD NOW, I'LL GO UP IN FLAMES.

BUT IF I DON'T, I CAN'T TAKE MY LEG APART AND I'LL SUFFOCATE IN HERE ANYWAY.

WHAT THE DEVIL DO I-?

...

25

BEAR! OVER HERE!

SOMEONE ELSE TOOK ADVANTAGE OF YOU AGAIN, EH?

SHAME ON YOU THIS TIME, BUT WILL YOU LEARN YOUR LESSON?

I MADE YOU THE VILLAIN OF MY STORY!

WILL YOU LET ME GET AWAY WITH IT?

STAND UP FOR YOURSELF! FIGHT ME! KILL ME IF YOU CAN-!

AH...
IT HURTS
MORE THAN I
THOUGHT IT
WOULD...

I WON'T
MAKE IT.

I'M
GOING TO
DIE AFTER
ALL—

27

28

I THOUGHT YOU WERE HAVING A GRAND OL' TIME WITH THAT NICK NINNY TAILOR...

PAH!

I HAVE THE NEEDLE NOW, SO I DON'T HAVE TO BOTHER WITH HIM ANYMORE.

YOU DIDN'T EXPECT ME TO FIGHT HIM WITH THOSE WATCHMEN AROUND, DID YOU? HE WAS A SORRY WHELP ON HIS OWN.

BESIDES YOU'RE STILL HANDY TO KEEP AROUND.

IF IT WEREN'T FOR YOU, I'D BE THE ONE CAUGHT IN THAT BEAR TRAP.

OH, I'M TOUCHED...

RRRRAAAAATHH!!!

GOODNESS!

WHAT A GHASTLY SOUND! WHAT WAS THAT?

HEH...

PETER

ARE YOU STILL WITH ME?

I MET A KINDRED SPIRIT TODAY...

OOOW!

GOD'S WOUNDS!

MOTHER OF MARY!

I'M BACK! I HAVE MORE WINE IF YOU NEED IT.

FOR HEAVEN'S SAKE. WHAT TOOK YOU SO LONG?

IT'S A NICE DAY. I THOUGHT I'D ENJOY IT.

THE SKIES AREN'T SO SUNNY FOR ALL OF US.

YOU WOULDN'T BE SO CHIPPER IF YOU WERE STITCHING UP YOUR OWN LEG.

WELL! THERE'S NO USE CRYING OVER THE MILK SOMEONE ELSE SPILLED, I ALWAYS SAY.

YOU KNOW...

...AT THIS RATE, YOU'LL END UP WITH A WHOLE BODY MADE OF WOOD ANYWAY.

HA. I'D RATHER LOSE ALL MY LIMBS THAN BECOME A PUPPET AGAIN.

31

TAMING YOU
BY GRACE PARK

I HOLD NO DELUSIONS ABOUT WHO HE IS. I KNOW HE'S A HUNTER.

I DON'T NEED ANY HARD EVIDENCE WHEN MY INSTINCTS WARN ME TO RUN.

BUT MY HEAD AND HEART BEG TO DIFFER SO INSTEAD, I JUST DOUBT ALL THE TIME.

AM I A MONSTER TAMED BY TRUE LOVE?

OR IS THIS A LONG HUNT?

IF I WERE TO BE BLINDSIDED WHILE IN THIS WEAKER FORM...

35

CAN'T I COME WITH YOU? I'M GOING TO BE SO BORED ALL BY MYSELF...

SORRY BABE, THEY'LL KILL ME IF I BREAK THE NO SIGNIFICANT OTHERS AT THE REUNION RULE.

YOU CAN MEET ALL MY BORING COLLEGE FRIENDS TOMORROW IF YOU WANT?

BUT TOMORROW—

WHY PAUL, WHAT'S SO SPECIAL ABOUT TOMORROW?

ARE YOU SERIOUS—!

I DEFINITELY DIDN'T MAKE A 7 O'CLOCK RESERVATION FOR OUR ANNIVERSARY AT THAT FANCY ITALIAN PLACE—

YOU'RE A DICK.

I LOVE YOU!

LOVE YOU TOO.

MIGHT BE HOME A LITTLE LATE, SO DON'T WAIT UP FOR ME!

SIX MONTHS.

PAUL AND I ARE VERY HAPPY.

BUT HAPPINESS CAN'T FEED HUNGER.

I'M SURE HE KNOWS, OR AT LEAST SUSPECTS WHAT I REALLY AM.

SO I FIND OUT TONIGHT. DOES HE LOVE ME ENOUGH TO TURN A BLIND EYE?

OR DOES HE FOLLOW ME RIGHT NOW?

TO CATCH ME IN THE ACT?

I WONDER IF HE'S HOPING THAT HE'S TAMED ME?

OR IF HE'S EAGER TO FINALLY START THE HUNT...

I GREET MY FRIENDS—

AND FELLOW PREDATORS.

THOUGH WE PREFER TO HUNT ALONE, WE'RE STILL A COMMUNITY.

WE GIVE EACH OTHER ALIBIS TO BLEND IN WITH OUR PREY.

THE ELEMENTS DON'T BOTHER ME IN THIS FORM.

THE ONLY THING I FEEL IS THE GNAWING PIT IN MY STOMACH.

PREY.

FAMILIES ARE ALWAYS CHOICE SELECTIONS.

AND SIX MONTHS OF FASTING HAS WHET MY APPETITE.

A GOOD HUNT DULLS THE SENSES SOMEWHAT,

BUT I STILL SMELL HIM APPROCHING...

AND THE BLOOD...

ISN'T HUMAN.

YOU...

...KILLED THEM.

YOU ACTUALLY CARE?

THEY WERE MY FRIENDS...

BUT I'M HAPPIER YOU SURVIVED.

41

PTEWPTEWPTEW

FWUMP

44

FWUMPH

CRRRPNK
CRRAK

AH.

SO HE REALLY
DID LOVE ME.

I'M SO HAPPY.

I WAS ABLE
TO TAME HIM.

plip

plip

...I SHOULD PROBABLY
CANCEL TOMORROW'S
DINNER RESERVATION.

COPING
MECHANISM
URSULA WOOD & JENN DOYLE

I HAVEN'T BEEN BACK HERE IN YEARS.

THERE YOU GO ...

I DON'T KNOW IF IT REALLY MATTERS, BUT BEST KEEP YOU NICE AND WARM!

HE LOVED YOU VERY MUCH.

AH

SOB HIC SOB HIC HIC

NEVER AGAIN WOULD HAVE BEEN TOO SOON –

– BUT I'M OUT OF IDEAS.

-BIP-

PLEASE,

HAVE A SEAT.

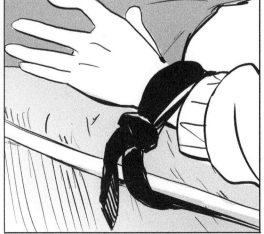

53

FWUMP

OKAY, LET'S SEE WHAT'S UNDER THERE.

CRAK

WHAT ARE YOU DOING?

JUST GIVING YOU A NEW PAINT JOB.

CLK

WOULD YOU FIND IT HELPFUL TO DO A BREATHING EXERCISE WITH ME?

NO -- SHUT UP.

OKAY.

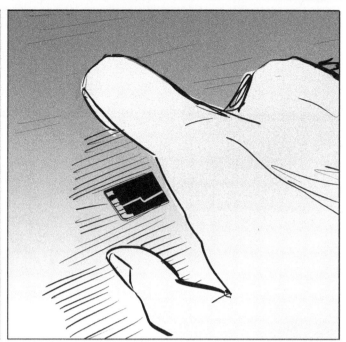

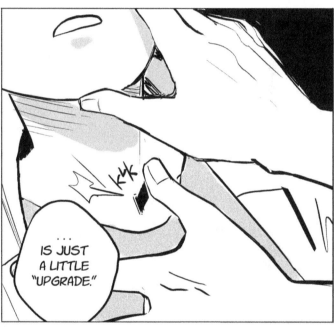

55

HEY, DUMMY.

WHAT'S UP?

NOT MUCH. WHERE ARE WE?

DON'T WORRY ABOUT IT.

WHAT'S THE LAST THING YOU REMEMBER?

UHHHHHHHH...

SCHOOL?

HM.

HAHA, WHAT?

IS THERE A WRONG ANSWER?

YO, AM I TIED TO THIS?

KINDA.

JUST PLAY ALONG, OKAY?

YOU WON'T REMEMBER THIS LATER.

HEY, ARE YOU OKAY?

YOU SEEM, I DON'T KNOW, STRESSED...?

...

YOU NEVER NOTICE STUFF LIKE THAT.

56

SOR-RY.

DOESN'T MATTER.

WHO'S THIS?

THAT'S MOM.

TELL ME ABOUT THIS PICTURE.

THAT WAS AT THE STATE FAIR.

SHE WAS SCARED TO GO ON THE ROLLER COASTERS, BUT THEN --

SHE LIKED IT WHEN SHE TRIED IT.

I WISH ...

I WISH IT HADN'T COME TO THIS.

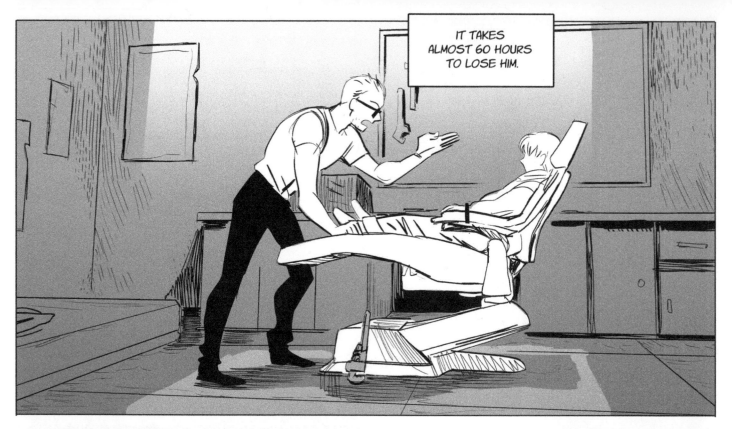

IT TAKES ALMOST 60 HOURS TO LOSE HIM.

HOW DOES EVERY QUESTION I ASK

MAKE HIM LESS HIMSELF?

WHO'S IN THIS PICTURE?

THAT'S YOU.

AND?

AND... ME.

SAY IT LIKE YOU MEAN IT!

...

HE LOVED YOU VERY MUCH.

heh

59

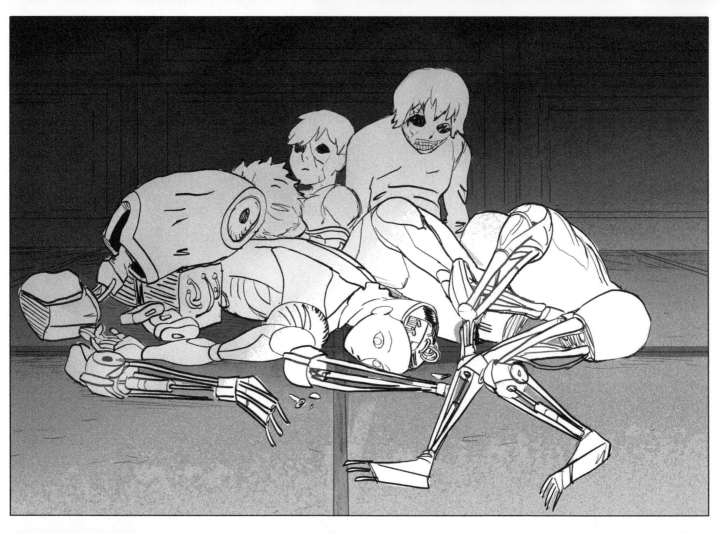

I CAN ALWAYS
TRY AGAIN.

END

63

TINCTURE

By Julie Wright

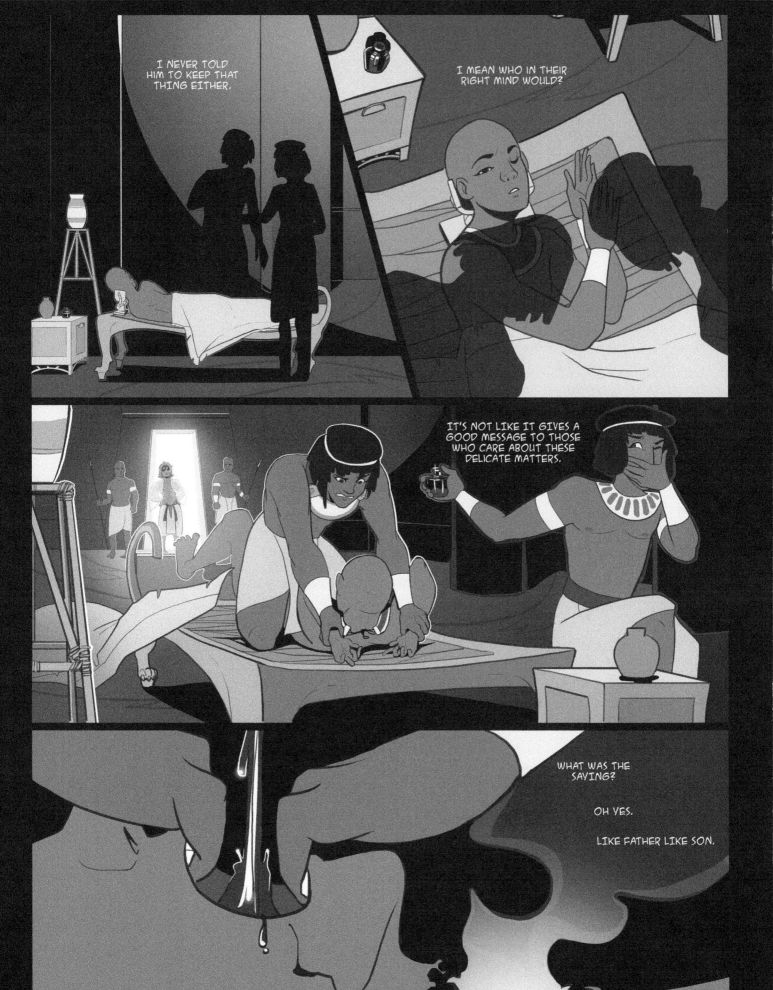

68

NOW STRENGTH WITHOUT POWER? THAT'S ALWAYS A SAD SIGHT.

I COULDN'T HELP BUT OFFER MY SERVICES TO THESE TWO.

BEING POWERFUL AND KNOWING NO LIMIT AND BEING POWERFUL AND KNOWING WHEN TO STOP SOUNDED LIKE AN EASY CHOICE TO ME.

BUT YOU CAN'T KNOW ANYTHING WHEN YOU'VE BEATEN ONE ANOTHER TO DEATH.

MAN ALWAYS SEEM TO FALL FOR THIS ONE.

BOREDOM OFTEN LEADS TO
EXCESS FOR THOSE WHO HAVE
THE LUXURY. NOW I DID TELL HER
TO KEEP HER HOBBIES TO
HERSELF LEST SHE GOT IN
OVER HER HEAD.

NOW STEALING FROM THE
SLAUGHTER HOUSE? I LET THE
WAR UNFOLD ITSELF BUT I DID
GIVE HIM THE OPTION TO LEAVE
HIS CAPTORS WITH A SMILE ON
HIS FACE.

71

PERFORMANCE ANXIETY IS TYPICAL. SOMETIMES YOU JUST NEED SOMETHING TO SLOW YOU DOWN TO COPE WITH ALL THE SCREAMING.

AFTER A WHILE, SHE JUST STOPPED COMPLETELY.

NOW WHAT DO WE HAVE HERE?

RARELY I RUN INTO THESE TYPES.

ALL SELFLESS AND INFURIATING.

I SHOULD FIND A SHELTER. I HOPE YOU AND YOUR DRINK HAVE A GOOD NIGHT.

I CAN'T EVEN REMEMBER THE LAST TIME SOMEONE RESISTED MY "ADVICE".

BUT...

HEY! YOU FORGOT THIS.

THESE TYPES ARE THE BEST SIGHT WHEN BROKEN.

74

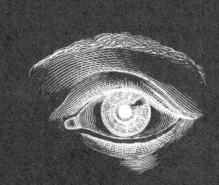

C-259

BY NECHAMA FRIER

DON'T LOOK SO DOWN.

WE'LL JUST...WIN, SOMEHOW.

IT'S SAD. WE DON'T EVEN KNOW WHAT IT REALLY IS...

WHEN I FIRST SAW IT COMING...

I REMEMBER THINKING... "HERE'S OUR REWARD".

IF WE DIE, IT'LL BE IN EACH OTHER'S ARMS.

HEY.

THAT'S SOMETHING RIGHT?

78

YES.

THAT REALLY IS SOMETHING.

WHAT A JOKE.

I'M JUST GOING TO DIE A LITTLE SOONER THAN THE REST.

RATS, ALL OF US.

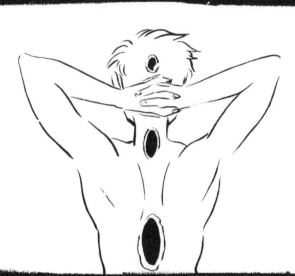

A KILLER.

NARCISSIST.

A SIMPLE BEAST OF PASSION.

...AND NONE GREATER OR MORE PATHETIC THAN I,

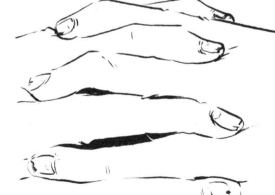

HANDS IN THE AIR, SAWICKI.

ALL YOU CAN DO IS SURRENDER.

83

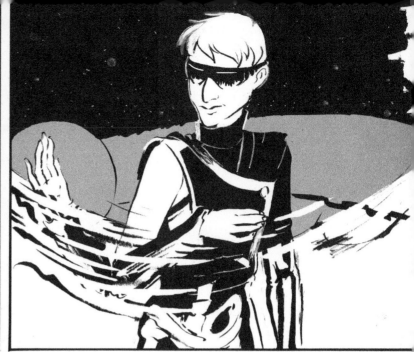

NO.

I HAVE A LITTLE MORE.

89

C-259 WAS BUILT ON A MOON CLOSE ENOUGH
TO AIDEV-8 TO SUSTAIN HUMAN LIFE
WHEN OUR LAST SHIP RAN OUT OF FUEL
FOURTEEN YEARS AND FIVE MONTHS AGO.

OUR FIRST NATIVE BABIES HAD BEEN BORN
THREE MONTHS BEFORE THE INVASION.

SEVEN GREENHOUSES HAD
BEGUN TO YIELD CROPS

C'MON, FILIP. FEEL A LITTLE GUILTY.

WHY?

FOR FUN.

CHRrrrIIIIIIIII

COMMANDER AEXELLE GALHAT SKATUS HAS ARRIVED, SIR.

GLK

CERTAINLY DOES SO WHENEVER HE FEELS LIKE IT...

HMHSSSS

PARDON ME—

AT EASE, SAWICKI. ARE YOU WELL?

SSSSSH—

THE MONITOR SAID YOU WERE IN A MEETING.

IT IS SO.

HAVE A SEAT.

WHY WOULDN'T I?

I DISAPPROVED WHEN YOU REFUSED MEDICAL ASSISTANCE AFTER YOUR VIOLENT ABERRATION FOUR TURNS AGO.

BUT IT OCCURS TO ME YOUR INJURIES MAY BE MENTAL RATHER THAN PHYSICAL.

THAT'S... THOUGHTFUL, BUT—

ARE YOU IN DISTRESS BECAUSE YOU ARE THE LAST HUMAN?

...e afterno... ...d a female of eight years of age i... ...enough con...ion ...t. most ...flesh has ... ...inedible because of disease or chemicals, ...relatively young age of ...lite of the force have decided to de- ...experiment with preparati... ...nits is still at large, although they are still believed to be deceased ...nce that some outdoor gear enabling ...ive in the surface ...ere are other factors such as low atmo- ...ther from the fo... ...make it difficult for humans to survive ...s. if you wish ...dates on the identities and fate of the ...ntinue now. ...or your response. . . . i did not hear a ...ve this story ...you change your mind later, please speak ...ews back to you ...new dissections have completed the medi- ...oon to be categ... ...ered and then extinct species. master filip ...ll be ...y different classification than the other ...in the ...ltanian research faction. aration. one of the ...lth... ...e still ... ...be deceased ...houg...ere

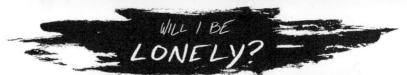

THE DEVIL'S PUPIL

ASHLEY MCCAMMON

I CAN NO LONGER COUNT THE NUMBER OF TIMES I HAVE CRAWLED FROM THIS PIT.

SPLSH

"THE DEVIL'S SCHOOL", THEY CALLED IT, ONCE.

AND I, HIS FAITHFUL STUDENT.

103

104

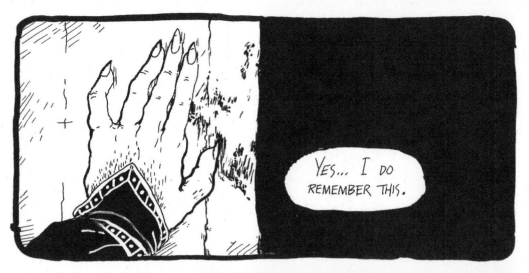

NEVER DO THEY SEE THE POWER THAT I HOLD...

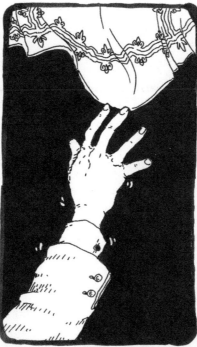

THEY DO NOT SEE WHAT IT IS THAT I OFFER.

I HAVE SOLD ALL BUT MY NAME IN AN EFFORT TO EXIST.

IT WAS A MATTER OF SURVIVAL, ONCE — AND STILL MET WITH SCORN, DISTRUST.

IT IS A SIMPLE PRICE OF BLOOD --

BUT IT WOULD SEEM THEY CANNOT PAY WITHOUT FEELING THEY WERE CHEATED.

110

119

122

ARE THE REFRESHMENTS TO YOUR SATISFACTION? IS THE TEMPERATURE IN THE ROOM COMFORTABLE FOR YOU . . .?
ARE YOU QUITE PLEASED WITH YOURSELVES . . . ?
ARE YOU CONTENT TO PUT THIS COMPANY INTO HANDS WITH THREE YEARS OF EXPERIENCE AS OPPOSED TO, SAY, THREE DECADES?
BECAUSE SHE IS MALLEABLE . . . BECAUSE SHE IS WEAK . . .
. . . BECAUSE SHE CAN BE SHAPED ACCORDING TO YOUR WHIMS . . .
. . . AND CONTROLLED.

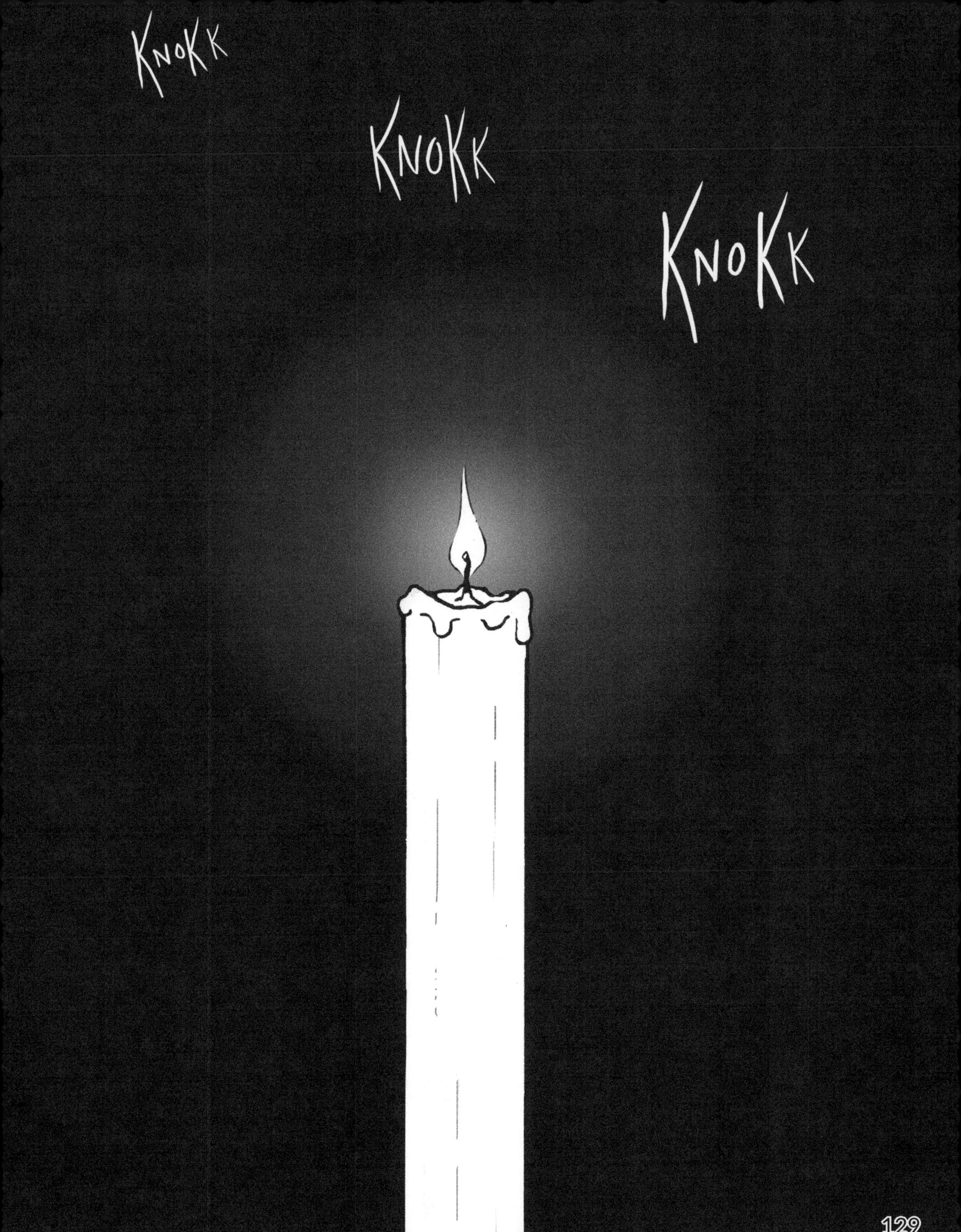
KNOKK
KNOKK
KNOKK

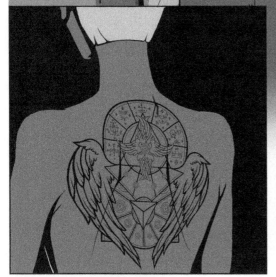

130

The Anima Sola.

An original, from the reknowned painter, Di Rocco.

Oh... Ah, pardon me. I'm Constable Warren, and you must be--

131

Sister Fortuna, yes.

Welcome to the House of the Immaculate.

Thank you for seeing me so unannounced, Sister.

I've... heard a lot about your establishment, but never much about what actually goes on here.

Then you are aware of the strict policy of confidentiality we implement within our walls.

Yes Sister, but you see--

I see you are not in uniform, Constable. That makes this a personal visit.

Ah... Yes, actually. You must have heard about the recent murders in the area.

All six victims were... beaten to death by someone's bare fists.

132

The only connection between the victims is that they had all... done business here.

My niece was one of them...

Half of the city has done business at this House. I suspect that is why you have yet to come up with a suitable warrant.

Please Sister! It's the only lead I have. Just a few questions! I-I'll pay if that's what it takes!

Hm.

In that case...

Since it is our duty to accommodate all of our patrons' needs, I will gladly show you around. This way, Constable.

Here, at the House of the Immaculate...

...We provide very special experiences that cater to our patrons' very specific needs.

Needs that would otherwise be frowned upon outside of these walls.

134

We live in a world plagued by the fear of eternal damnation. I am happy to provide relief and the freedom to be oneself to those who seek it.

It is not our job to judge.

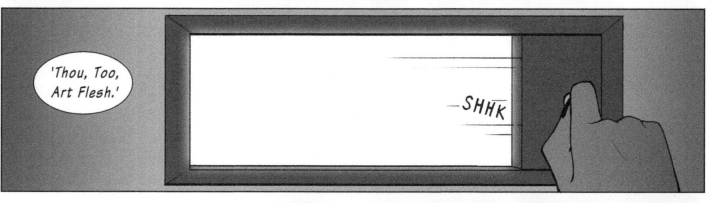

'Thou, Too, Art Flesh.'

—SHHK

It is against our natures to deny what we crave. We deny our own humanity in a foolish attempt to feel closer to the Divine.

Here, we celebrate what it means to be human. We embrace it without shame, free from the oppression of society.

'Sin' is a term invented by man. Our God does not judge us for what He made us to be.

After you.

What exactly was my niece doing in this place..?

For a police officer, you are far too trusting.

Excuse me?

BAMM

H-Hey!

What is this? I'm a police officer! You can't--

SHHK

We cater to all of our patrons' needs, here.

W-what? Ma'am-- A-ah, I mean, Sister! Open this door immediately! Y-you are obstructing an official investigation!

But I never put you on the investigation, Warren.

C-Commissioner Gransville??

Sir, W-what are you doing here?

138

I did not put you on the case due to your personal connection to one of the murder victims.

I gave you specific instructions not to look into it.

I knew your insolence would lead you to stick your nose where you're not suppose to.

Ksss

Ksshh

Your recklessness will get you killed.

Commissioner, sir! I'm sorry for disobeying...

...But we've gotten nowhere in the case for the past two months and each month that goes by there is one more found dead!

I'm desperate! We need to stop this senseless death! Any day now the killer might strike again!

I have to find the one who killed my--

KRAK

139

140

You've made quite the mess again, Commissioner.

Clean up costs extra.

Of course.

That includes the replacement of the rug.

Yes. I'm aware.

141

t.s.s.s.

End.

STRIKER

Hey, they're here!

147

Let's have a good game today!

Just like old times?

...

Call it.

Heads.

Dempsey, get in position.

FWEET!

We need to cover that guy!

nod nod

Over here!

What the-?!

150

153

All of you need to *step up* or my hard work will go to waste!

Um, Johnson?

Can I have a chance? My parents are here, and I want to do something cool like you!

They never mak[e] to my games ar[e]

You can't win this alone!

I have the perfect idea for you...

You're all doing great. Stay on top of Johnson! *Let's* win this!

154

What's with that face?

Leo!!

Now's my chance!

156

157

Did I do it right, Johnson?

You...!

What was it you said?

"You can't win alone?"

Good game.

TSK!

LITTLE GUARDIANS.

MAKE HASTE.

SPLOOSH

THEY CALL ME "EVIL".

IS THAT WHAT THEY THINK SURVIVAL IS?

EVERYTHING DIES.

IS THERE ANYTHING MORE NOBLE THAN PROVIDING LIFE FOR ANOTHER?

THWIP

THWIP

THERE WERE THOSE THAT DEPENDED UPON ME.

TO THEM, I WAS JUST "QUEEN".

IF IT'S EVIL THEY WANT

THEN THAT'S WHAT THEY SHALL GET.

THUD!

THUD!

WOOSH...

I WILL HAVE VENGEANCE.

167

I WILL NOT BOW TO NAÏVETY!

THUMP
THUMP

From the NEKOMATA

When a cat grows old,

and his tail grows too long...

it will split into two tails.

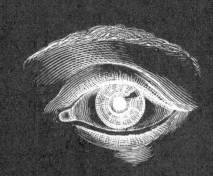

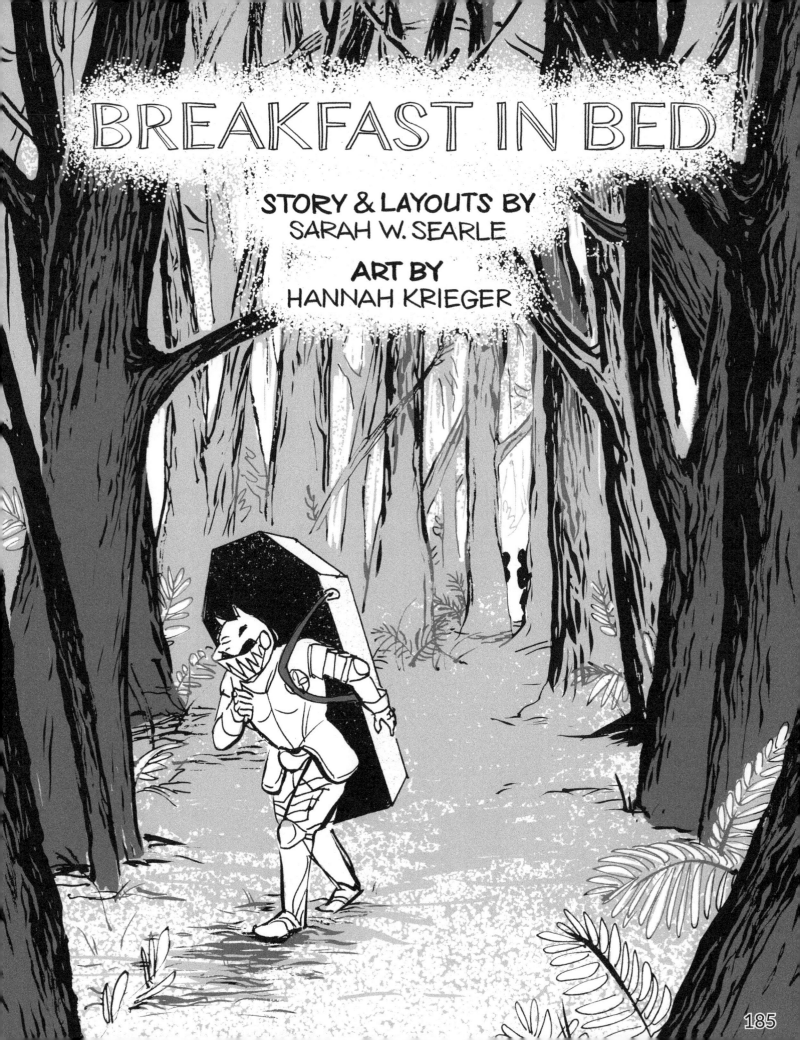

WHAT KIND OF WEIRDO LUGS A COFFIN AROUND?

IT'S A *DECOY.*

HE'S HIDING SOMETHING VALUABLE IN IT, AND WE'RE GOING TO FIND OUT WHAT.

AGH!!

AAAHHH!!

189

NO... PLEASE! HAVE MERCY!!

THE HELL DO YOU WANT?

TH—THE COFFIN! SHE THOUGHT M—MONEY WAS IN IT, OR—

BUFFOONS. THAT'S MY *HUSBAND* IN THERE.

S—S—SO SORRY!!

191

192

AND THEY LIVED
HAPPILY EVER AFTER.

The End.

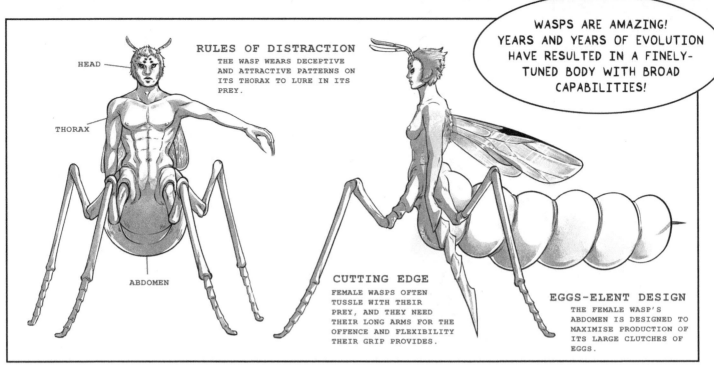

RULES OF DISTRACTION
THE WASP WEARS DECEPTIVE AND ATTRACTIVE PATTERNS ON ITS THORAX TO LURE IN ITS PREY.

HEAD

THORAX

ABDOMEN

CUTTING EDGE
FEMALE WASPS OFTEN TUSSLE WITH THEIR PREY, AND THEY NEED THEIR LONG ARMS FOR THE OFFENCE AND FLEXIBILITY THEIR GRIP PROVIDES.

EGGS-ELENT DESIGN
THE FEMALE WASP'S ABDOMEN IS DESIGNED TO MAXIMISE PRODUCTION OF ITS LARGE CLUTCHES OF EGGS.

WASPS ARE AMAZING! YEARS AND YEARS OF EVOLUTION HAVE RESULTED IN A FINELY-TUNED BODY WITH BROAD CAPABILITIES!

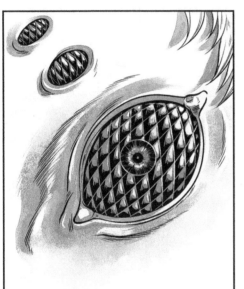

LIKE MANY OTHER INSECTS, WASPS HAVE LARGE COMPOUND EYES THAT GIVE THEM VERY LARGE FIELDS OF VISION, AND ALSO ALLOW THEM TO SEE FAST MOVEMENTS WITH GREAT PRECISION!

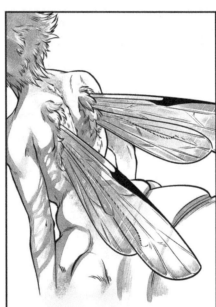

THE TWO PAIRS OF WINGS CAN BEAT AT SPEEDS OF OVER ONE HUNDRED TIMES PER SECOND, ALLOWING THEM TO CONTROL EXACTLY WHERE THEY FLY!

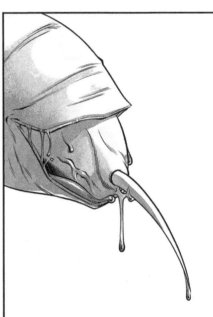

AND THE FEMALE BRACONID PROJECTS A VENOMOUS STINGER FROM HER REAR, WHICH DOUBLES AS AN OVIPOSITOR FOR LAYING HER EGGS!

IN FACT, THIS IS WHAT SETS BRACONID WASPS APART FROM OTHER WASP SPECIES!

BY FAR THE MOST FASCINATING THING ABOUT THESE WASPS --

198

IS THEIR METHOD OF REPRODUCTION!

UNLIKE A LOT OF DIFFERENT INSECTS, THE BRACONID WASP DOESN'T JUST LAY HER EGGS ANYWHERE, WHERE THEY COULD BE DAMAGED BY THE ENVIRONMENT OR EATEN BY OTHER CREATURES.

INSTEAD --

THE WASP SEARCHES OUT A LIVING HOST TO LAY HER EGGS IN!

MOST FEMALES, HOWEVER, ARE SUCCESSFUL IN THEIR EGGLAYING PROCESS, AND WILL TRANSPORT THE HOST AND HER PRECIOUS EGGS TO MORE FAMILIAR TERRITORY.

HER NEST.

THOUGH THESE WASPS DON'T HAVE A QUEEN, THEY OFTEN LIVE TOGETHER IN BIG COLONIES FOR SAFETY.

MALES WILL SPEND MOST OF THE TIME BUILDING THE NEST, WHILE FEMALES LEAVE THE NEST TO HUNT FOR PREY AND LAY THEIR EGGS.

202

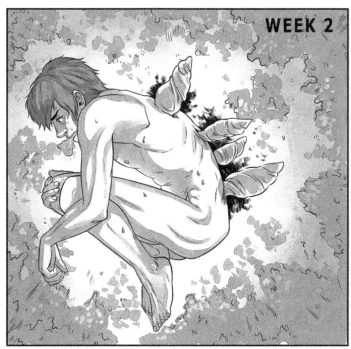

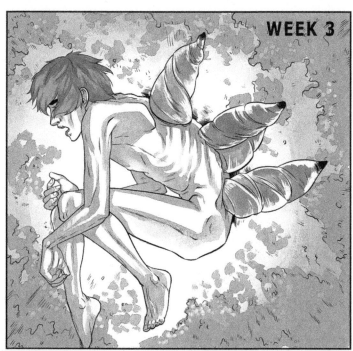

LOOK, THERE'S A BABY!

THE BABIES EAT THEIR WAY OUT OF THE HOST, AND THAT GIVES THEM THE ENERGY TO COMFORTABLY WALK AROUND AS SOON AS THEY'RE OUT IN THE OPEN. YOU GO, LITTLE GUY!

OF COURSE, THE FIRST THING THE YOUNG WASPS DO IS SEEK OUT THE FOOD CHAMBER, WHERE THE MATURE WASPS HAVE ALREADY STORED AWAY FOOD THAT THE YOUNG WASPS CAN EAT.

204

OF COURSE, ONCE THE WASP HAS SPENT SOME TIME MATURING, IT ALSO BEGINS LEAVING THE NEST TO EXPAND ITS FAMILY'S TERRITORY, AND LAY EGGS.

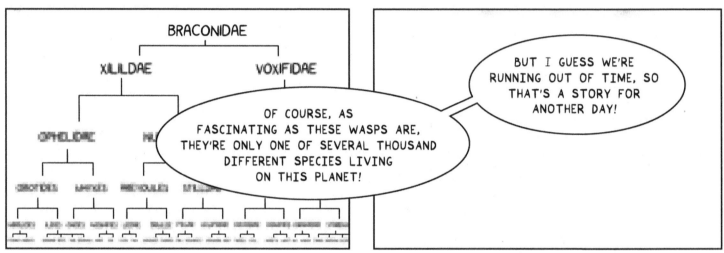

PROCESS
WORK

SPIRACLES TO SHAKE FIRE

Glass Chain mail?

TEN VAN WINKLE, "GLASKÖNIGIN"
Early character concepts.

Originally, the Queen in "Glaskönigin" was going to be a Prince trying to rescue his lover. Along the way, the Prince became a Princess, and then the lover became a sister. The way I see it, I know plenty of people who would ditch their romantic obligations, but it takes an extra-slimey person to let a family member burn...

THE BEAR AND THE JESTER
CHARACTER NOTES
and other unhelpful comments

Pietro

Pietro's lines are curly, slanted, but not harshly angular. He has a snaky grace to him. His facial features are mostly pointed.

...

When emphasizing an expression, his lip protrudes and/or his gums are visible. The teeth are also often showing.

He emotes mostly through his mouth and tends to make "sneery" expressions.

Pietro's not meant to be good-looking, but he's not without a certain charm of his own.

Hey! I know a left-handed compliment when I see it. Get that outta here!

Pietro is vulnerable in a way that Scissors isn't. (Both in a physical and emotional sense.) To me, that's the main difference between the two characters!

His eyes are hooded, but deceptively large because something about him has to look engaging.

The 'Scissor Man'

Scissors' personality is 'deceptively amiable,' so he's a mix of friendly square shapes and harsher triangles.

His body is blocky, tall, and seemingly immovable. But he quickly becomes looming (and scary!) when the situation calls for it.

His hands are often in his pockets so he looks harmless. Don't fall for it.

His eyes are only visible during specific moments —whenever there's a genuine emotion coming from him, or a sentiment I want to make clear to the reader.

The Tailor

His outfit is loosely based off 17th century Netherlandish clothing. I wanted him to look frail, but without the gangly wiliness that Pietro has.

Since Fate has dubbed him the 'good guy,' the Tailor is used to things going his way and has become sub-consciously entitled. So I pushed up his nose for a snobby look.

I don't think he's actually clever. He was good at one thing and his reputation was blown out of proportion.

Thanks for reading!
-ENOCH

211

"Is this not distressing for you?"

NECHAMA FRIER, "C-259"
Early storyboards.
NEXT PAGE:
Character concepts; fashion sketches.

"I'm not a sentimental individual."

COLONY   OCCUPATION

213

Thou Too,
Art Flesh.

The House of the Immaculate

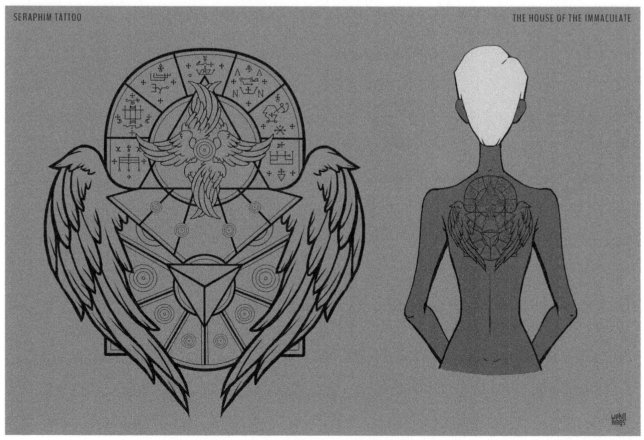

ASHLEY MCCAMMON, "THE DEVIL'S PUPIL"
Character art.
NEXT PAGE:
Storyboards, style tests, and outfit concepts.

217

TIM STOWELL, STEPH STOBER,
SHAZZBAA, "STRIKER"
Storyboards.
NEXT PAGE:
Character height chart.

ST. ABRAHAM ACADEMY'S SHARKS

JOHNSON   CLARK   DEMPSEY

COLONIAL HIGH SCHOOL'S TIGERS

LEO   GARCIA   IRWIN

Witchweed

CONCEPT & DESIGN

I was and will always be a Sailor Moon fan. I rooted for her when I was young, but with the recent reboot, I approached the show from a more mature perspective. I was closer in age (technically) to Beryl than Usagi. All this love and justice was a lot harder to swallow the second time around. I wanted to get in touch with my inner evil Queen.

Taking a page from Takeuchi Naoko, the creator of Sailor Moon, I was inspired by high fashion for the design of my Evil Queen. I turned to the Savage Beauty Collection by Alexander McQueen. So many of his pieces are works of fantasy with a sense of drama I wanted for my character.

t took a few tries to get the right look, to be referential without blatantly copying. These are sketches that culminated in her final design

A NOTE FROM THE "COPING MECHANISM" SCRIPTWRITER:

Every creative team has its own process. When Jenn Doyle and I collaborate on a comic, it's a little more complicated than one of us drawing and the other writing, though of course we each have our specialty. As a point of interest, I've streamlined our process down to five essential steps:

1. We work together to establish the story beats and visual aesthetic of our piece. ("Cyberpunk Erlking" was our concept for this one.)

2. I write a script that breaks the action down into pages and panels. I think there's an official format for comics scripts, but my system is clear and easy to edit, so it's chill.

3. I use a pencil and legal pad to draw utilitarian thumbnails that show how I imagined the layout and blocking.

4. Jenn takes this monstrous storyboard from my feeble hands and transforms it into a sensual feast for the eyes, correcting choices that are "physically impossible" or "very ugly" and adding features such as "perspective" and "legs."

5. I come up with a pun-based title at the last minute.

What you're looking at here at is the massive, massive difference between steps 3 and 4. If there's a lesson to be learned here, it is probably that artists are witches.

Enjoy!
URSULA WOOD

AFTERWORD

I've never been a sound hand at staying away from the bad guys. I pride myself on writing good characters from time to isolated time, but the majority of my characters are awful, abhorrent jackasses who commit anything from minor misdemeanors to atrocities on a weekly basis. I spend a lot of time puzzling over this fictional realm within myself—my characters' dedication to being terrible is like a mirror image of my real efforts to be good, really good, to the best of my abilities.

In essence, I'm trying to answer the question most often posed to **VERTOSCOPE** since it's inception, which has been *why*? Why villains, and why is it so important to focus on them like this? Fiction needs flavor, contrast, and daring. Fiction is our safety zone to dive into a pool of slumbering darkness and untangle unseen twists. As women creators, as queer creators, as racially and culturally diverse creators, the team responsible for this book all poured their heart and soul into creating awful characters because the catharsis of fictional villainy is universal. Let's face it, living life can be exhausting, and at the end of the day I feel calm and at peace if I get to unwind with a terrific story about the people who decide to watch it all burn down.

Publishing this book is monumental to me. Up until this point I have entrusted my comic work to others, sometimes with incredible results, sometimes with crushing rejection. This book point-blank was motivated by it—not the bitterness or disappointment rejection brings, but the eventual realization that I had the chance to take fate into my hands.

I wanted to cultivate a collection that matches what I'm passionate about. Publishing **VERTOSCOPE** to me means taking control of all of my work, baring my soul fully to the public and passing that opportunity on to a number of my peers as well. Thank you for giving me the chance to share the results of this tumultuous journey with you—I hope you found a moment of true thrill in the process, perhaps quite a few.

When I consider my life and how art fits into and defines it, I often find myself at the same conclusion: I want a professional career in illustration, but I want to create comics for myself. Comics are a personal spot, a soft and vulnerable place in my armor. The personal categorization of comics as a work of passion pushes me all the harder to find opportunities to make them, to create opportunities for them to exist. The book you've just read is a result of that force, that need from us and our collaborators to make comics we want to see.

I hope to make more books like this. I hope to continue to grow as an artist and as a publisher. No matter what I want to continue to champion action and creativity in every aspect of my life—if there's something you need to make, make it. A story you need to tell, tell it. Make your mark on the world and take the time to look down on it fondly too. I'm a small fish in a big ocean trying to say big words, but they make sense to me, so I hope they do well by you too.

MOST OF ALL, THANK YOU,
NECHAMA FRIER

ACKNOWLEDGEMENT

Our sincere thanks to each and every one of our Kickstarter backers, since this book would not have happened without you. We want to extend special gratitude towards the following backers who pledged significantly in order to make **VERTOSCOPE** a reality:

- **Bottled Lightning**, the studio behind The Only Living Boy, High Moon, and Box 13, carries the credit of <u>Associate Producer</u>.
- **Marci Cancio-Bello**, co-founder of **Print-Oriented Bastards** and accomplished author/poet, who carries the credit of <u>Producer</u> for her amazing generosity.
- **Mary Nann,** with heartfelt thanks to her support of family and our future success in the arts.
- **Michelle Czajkowski**, the creator of webcomic **Ava's Demon** and an incredible force in the arts, will receive a custom comic along with her book thanks to her generosity.

Behind the scenes, the following powers of nature made contributions that couldn't go unrecognized:

- **Sarah W. Searle**, who in addition to providing an incredible comic script also offered that story for advanced publicity and got hands-on with our media campaign.
- **Luke Blackwood**, a one man film marvel who directed, shot, edited, and processed our Kickstarter video in just one night and day.
- **Jeff Moore**, who passionately supported our efforts and donated his time, transportation, and backstage appearances behind dark windows to make key operations possible.
- **Kath Hsi**, our ingenious designer, at whom we threw countless Gordian knots of Book Problems to witness with awe as she untangled them with what seemed like a magic touch. Our blog, campaign, and book have unique finesse thanks to her patient labor.

And to every supporter who blogged, tweeted, shared, or just plain chattered by word of mouth about the project until we reached goal—this book is also for you to be proud of.

CREDITS

LYNN NGUYEN (COVER ARTIST)

Lynn Nguyen is an illustrator and visual artist from Sydney, Australia. She enjoys folklore, scary stories, world-folk music, anime, and collecting old books and occult objects.

teeething.com

TEN VAN WINKLE

XVW reads, draws and writes comics from Ithaca, NY and disseminates her work on Twitter @tenny_boo.

xvw-art.tumblr.com

MADY G.

Mady G. is an illustrator and comics artist with a passion for horror, cooking, and 70's fashion. For added spice, they're also a professional voice actor!

madyg.com

ENOCH

C. Ann Gordon is s a freelance illustrator and comic artist based in Ontario, Canada. She's interested in using her knowledge of the narrative form to explore the potential of visual storytelling and create comics with emotional depth and novelistic qualities.

cgartportfolio.wordpress.com

GRACE PARK

Grace is a California-based SCAD graduate with a BFA in Sequential Arts and minor in Storyboarding. She loves all forms of storytelling, but comics are her passion (she'll also get emotional over fictional characters).

artingbygrace.tumblr.com

URSULA WOOD

Ursula Wood lives in Brooklyn and likes to think their eventual robot double will be treated well and have a nice time. Read their queer sci-fi romance serial below.

starlingstory.tumblr.com

JENN DOYLE

Jennifer Doyle lives in Brooklyn and works as an illustrator because being a cat unfortunately does not pay. Follow their webcomic about political intrigue and sexy murders below.

sparklermonthly.com/series/
knights-errant
knightserrantcomic.tumblr.com

ONE OF TWO

One of Two is a full time illustrator and comics artist with a passion for independent collaboration. She works together with Ama on their webcomic **Riven Seal**.

lesserkeystudios.com

NECHAMA FRIER

Nechama's passion for fictional misbehavior extends to her webcomic **Red Rabbit** and her illustration. Strike up a chat with her on Twitter at @NechamaFrier!

nechamafrier.com
redrabbitcomic.com

ASHLEY MCCAMMON

Ashley McCammon is a queer comic artist and illustrator from New Jersey.

avmccammon.com

FATE

Team FATE! is made up of Rainy and F. Lee. This collaborative duo makes comics individually and collaboratively. You can find their other work below.

frontandcentaur.com
FickleRed.com
fleebites.tumblr.com

SEY VEE

Sey watched too many horror movies as a kid, and now makes a living off of drawing creepy comics and characters who blur the lines between what is considered good and evil. In their free time, Sey enjoys collecting curiosities and singing to their bratty parrot.

wekillkings.tumblr.com

TIM STOWELL

Tim Stowell wears a lot of hats: programmer, improviser, podcast host, but **VERTOSCOPE** marks the first time he dons the writer hat since high school. He will continue to wear this hat throughout 2016 and beyond with several comic and game projects in development.

medium.com/@skeletim

STEPH STOBER

Steph Stober is a freelance illustrator, designer, and all-around fabulous cartoonist. You can read her completed webcomic **Final Arcanum** below.

stephstober.me
finalarcanum.com

SHAZZBAA

D. Shazzbaa Bennett is a webcomic artist with a simultaneous love of quirky upbeat friendships and Lovecraftian horrors. You can find her webcomic, **Runewriters**, which features both of these things below!

shazzbaa.com
runewriters.com

AMA

Ama is a scholar—a US native, but currently doing research abroad in both Japan and England. Ama collaborates with One of Two regularly on their webcomic **Riven Seal**.

amasugiru.tumblr.com

EMILEE MCGLORY

Emilee works full-time as a designer and somehow finds time to put out amazing comic work as well. She loves cartoons, the mechanical, and the slightly (or more than slightly) demented in her fiction.

cyclopticrobot.tumblr.com

SARAH WINIFRED SEARLE

Sarah Winifred Searle hails from spooky New England where she makes comics, pets cats, and haunts Twitter (@swinsea).

swinsea.com

HANNAH KRIEGER

Hannah Krieger is best known for her webcomic, **Camodad**. She hopes that her new webcomic, **Psychic Mansion**, will be up and running by the time this book is published.

hkrieger.com/Comics

FAL

Hal Preece is an illustrator and comic book artist living in England. He is currently working on his post-apocalyptic Japanese-language webcomic, **Vestige**, which is published online at MangaX.

cacoethic.tumblr.com

MIRU

A. 'Miru' Lee is a freelance comic artist located near Chicago. Her supernatural-action Japanese-language webcomic, **Welcome to Dietroit!**, is published online by MangaX.

inktrashing.tumblr.com